Pinocchio

Illustrated by Eric Kincaid

Brimax Books Newmarket England

Old Geppetto was making a puppet.

As he cut the wood he heard a voice.

"Please do not hurt me," it said.

Geppetto looked all around.

He could not see anyone so

he went on with his work.

When he made the puppet's eyes,
they moved. When he made the mouth,
it laughed. When he made the feet,
they kicked.
"You are just like a real boy,"
said Geppetto.
He called the puppet Pinocchio.

Geppetto showed
Pinocchio how
to walk.

Naughty Pinocchio ran into the
street. Geppetto ran after him.
A policeman thought Geppetto was
being unkind. He took Geppetto
to the police station.

Pinocchio went home. He was very
pleased with himself.
"Boys who run away are sorry
in the end," said a talking
cricket. Pinocchio threw a hammer
at the cricket.
"I am taking no notice of you,"
he said.

Pinocchio went out
in the rain to
find some food.
Nobody would give
him any. He went
home hungry. He sat
by the fire and
fell asleep.

Geppetto knocked at
the door. Pinocchio
got up to answer it.
He fell to the floor.
"The fire has eaten
my feet," he cried.

Geppetto climbed in through the window.

"Don't worry, Pinocchio," said Geppetto. "I will make you some new feet. First we shall have something to eat."

Pinocchio was very pleased with
his new feet.
"I shall go to school and make you
proud of me," he said to Geppetto.
"But I need a reading book."
Geppetto sold his coat to buy
the reading book.

On his way to school Pinocchio saw
a puppet theatre. He sold his book
and paid to go in. He forgot all
about school. He stayed all day
and all night.

The puppet man gave him five
gold coins to take home.

On the way home Pinocchio met
a fox and a cat. The fox pretended
to be lame. The cat pretended
to be blind. They tried to trick
Pinocchio out of his gold coins.
Pinocchio ran away from them.

The fox and the
cat chased him.
They caught him
and tied him
to a tree.

He was rescued
by a fairy. She
took him home.
"How did this
happen?" she asked.

Pinocchio started to tell her the truth but he said he had lost the five gold coins. They were not lost. They were in his pocket. His nose began to grow.

His nose grew because he was telling lies.

His nose grew
very long indeed.
He could not
get it through
the door.
At last the fairy took pity on him.
She called some woodpeckers. The
woodpeckers pecked his nose back
to the right size.

Pinocchio wanted to see Geppetto.
"I shall go home now," said
Pinocchio. On the way he met
the fox and the cat. This time they
stole his money. Pinocchio told
a policeman. The policeman did not
believe him. He put Pinocchio
in prison.

A long time later Pinocchio came out of prison. He went looking for Geppetto again. Geppetto was looking for Pinocchio. He went to sea in a boat.

Pinocchio went to the seashore. He saw Geppetto's boat tossed on the waves. He swam out to help him.

Pinocchio met a dolphin in the sea.
"Geppetto has been swallowed by
a sea monster," said the dolphin.
Pinocchio sadly swam on. He
reached an island and met the fairy.
"I don't want to be a puppet," said
Pinocchio. "I want to be a boy."
"You can be a boy if you are good,"
said the fairy. "First you must
go to school."

Pinocchio tried to be good but
it was too hard. He ran away
to Toyland with some other naughty
boys. In Toyland they were all
so lazy they soon turned into
donkeys. Pinocchio was sold
to a circus. In the circus ring
Pinocchio fell and hurt his leg.

He was thrown into the sea to drown. But he turned back into a puppet. A sea monster swallowed him.

What a surprise! There inside the fish Pinocchio found Geppetto. They hugged each other.

"We can escape when the monster is asleep," said Pinocchio. They swam out of the monster's mouth. From that day on Pinocchio looked after Geppetto. Finally the fairy granted his wish. She made him into a real boy.

All these appear in the pages of
the story. Can you find them?

Geppetto

Pinocchio

fox

cat